The Still Collection

By,
Justin Keith

Dedicated To:

Judy and Jerry Beathard

Jimmy and Valarie Keith

And my little brother Caleb Keith

Table of Contents

The Time Travel Series

Empty Entity (Time Travel Part 1)

Absorbing time crystals
Grasping empty space
Like an infant
With its blanket
Awaiting protecting embrace

Looking back at what was left
Floating still and somber
Listening to what can not be seen
Bringing forth an empty entity
Creating a space even smaller

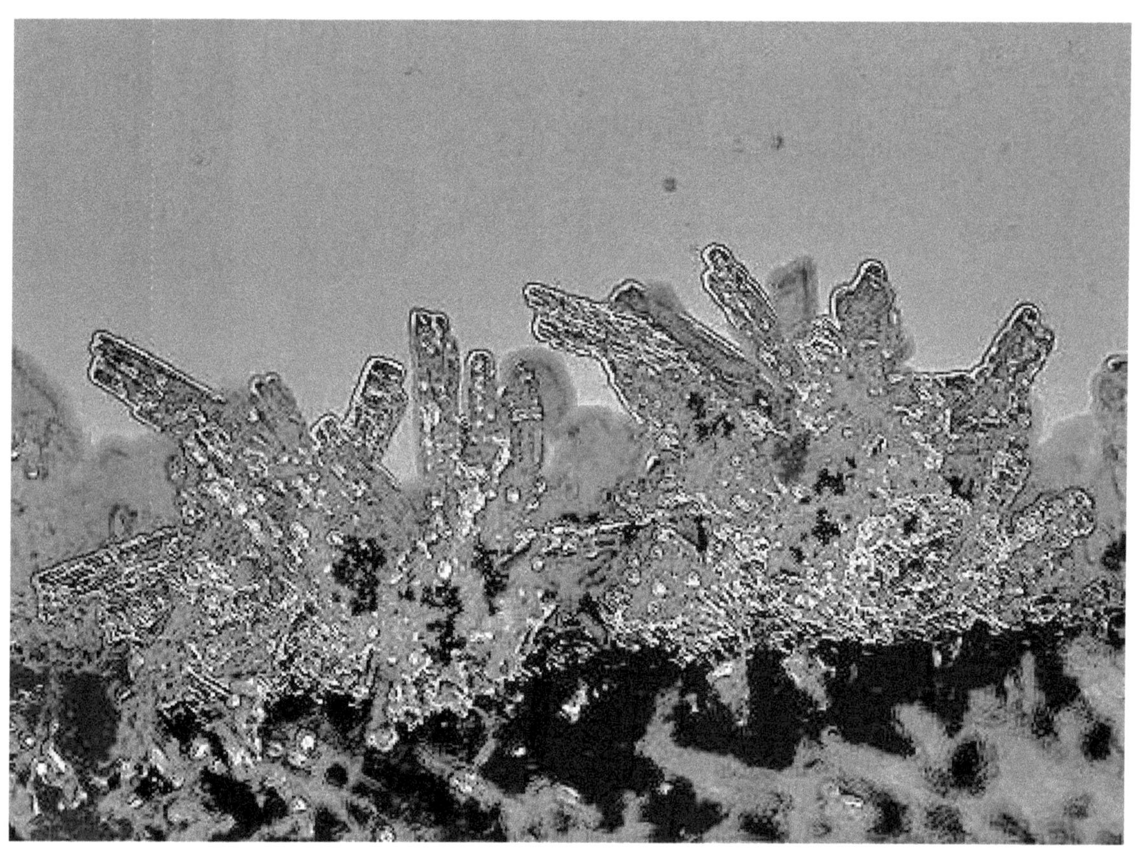

The Hollow Crystals (Time Travel Part 2)

The crystals that grew
Inside the cave at night
Had no reasons
Hadn't any thinking
They just grew
Expanding
Waiting as the years passed
And then the harvest
Mined for and collected
Inside that deep dark cave
Taken by surprise
And emptied of their souls
Until the moons light hit
And then filled with life

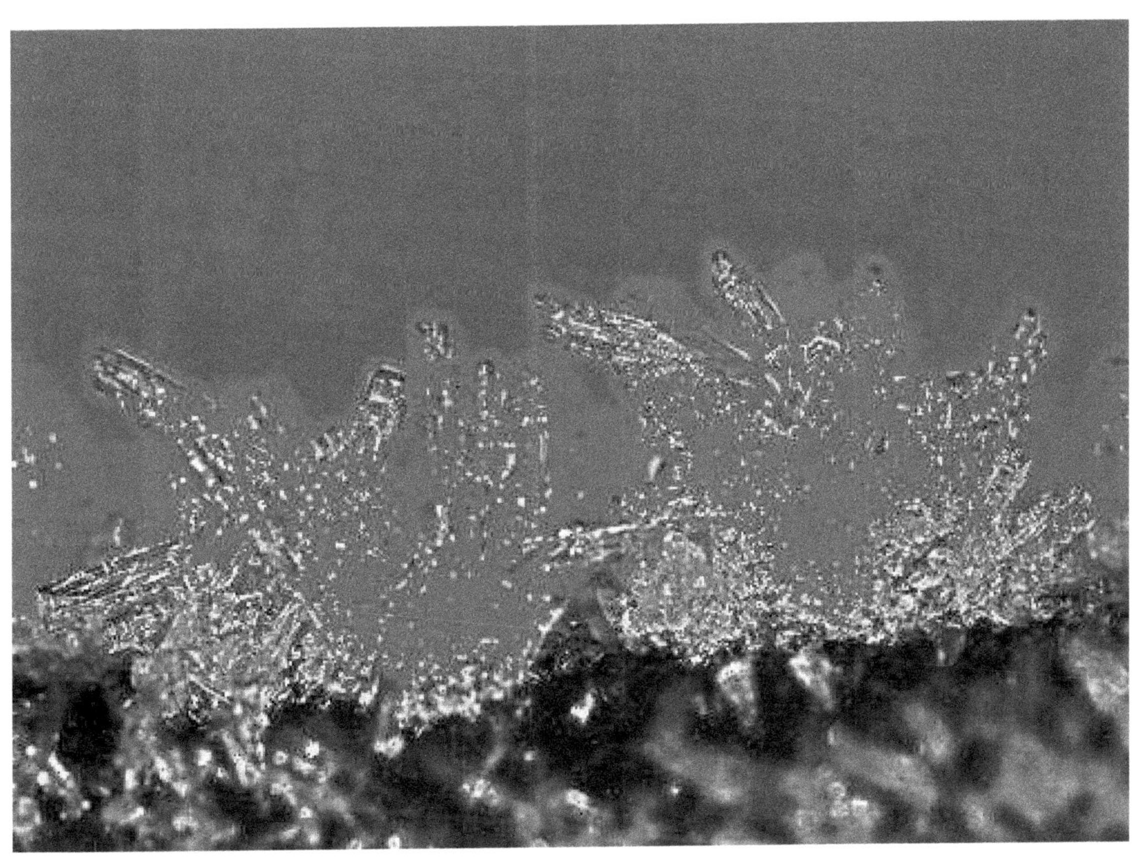

Experience the Experiment (Time travel Part 3)

Walk inside
Step through
Enter unknown
Leap of faith
Sudden movement
Vision obscured
Hearing impaired
Shaking rapid
Seizure trauma
Light replaced
Only darkness
Mysteries unfolding
Glass shatters
Crystals hold
Empty entity
Getting smaller
There is the light
I see the light
I move it with my mind
I am in complete control

The Field of Glass (Time Travel Part 4)

A field of glass breaks
Wondering what is next
Hoping for the best
But then another mistake

The space getting smaller
Time crystals never knew
What hope really can do
The shadow never falters

Time Travel is Inevitable (The Conclusion)

Reaching the end
I pass through the lines
The universe becomes unstable
It loses all control

There is much I have learned
The burning stars I can't deny
Rockets fly away
As space disappears

Nothing is nothing
And it can not be measured
The time crystals are there
But the shadows are not

End of the Time Travel Series

Food for the Lion

The lion that would roar
Just before
An attack
They all ran in a pack
All but one who was lost
He had the oddest thought
He would stay behind
And wait for the lion to find
And then they would meet
Before meat

Night Falls

The night falls, and
The stars awake from the days spell
To watch the world from above
Until the nights journey reaches its end
Until the sun starts to sing its song
To give birth to a new day
And see it off
As the night pulls it away

The Wave

The ground shook
And then it stopped
We thought it was over
But it was not

The wave came
And it crashed
It filled the streets
It all happened so fast

The Great Wonders of Space

Everyone stood up and waved
That day
At that giant in space
He was just passing by
That day
The day that everything changed
The sun did not reach us
That day
We were covered in darkness
There weren’t any questions
That day
There wouldn’t have been any answers
They threw us away
They say
We were left alone in space

THE KOVU CHRONICLES
Book One – The Great Escape

In an instant my room was filled with bright white lights and I awoke the very moment that it was. It must've been morning, but I wondered if it really was. I often ask myself these questions of the outside world just to try to satisfy my always hungry interest. My curiosity begs for answers so that it may be put out of its misery.

Of course my mind never gives itself any answers to the questions that I relentlessly torture it with, and I wouldn't dare create my own for if I did there would always be that small amount of doubt that would stay there stuck like a frozen pixel in my brain. I would scratch, eat, tear, and throw my own self up out of pure disgust for what I would have created, and what I would've created would have come straight from my own imagination which would make it part of my inner self. If I knew that it was a part of me and I the reason why so, I would then proceed to destroy everything that is to my existence until I found myself barely hanging with much well deserved self-intent on the cliff of suicide.

I am not mad. I am not insane, nor crazy. My mind may be a little far off, a little lost from its home on the throne, but that is only because the kingdom has been clouded, and quite crowded with all these fierce terrifying dragons flying about freely.

The white coats have done this to me with all their needles, knives, scalpels, and let me not forget the strange tools they have used to make me sickened with terrible terrible disease, and then make pretend with jolly happy persona switch over and comforting soft sleep like voice change. Every time I lay my eyes on these white coats it's as if I pull back the curtains and reveal a brilliantly collected and organized how-to on how the tricksters are to lay the cards on the not so friendly manipulative table.

I have wasted too much time already, they shall be most infuriated if I find myself late-fashion to class, no matter how stream eyed, no exception still. I have already hopped from my dream-vessel and on to my not-so-human feet, how strange. Enter reality, or maybe perhaps bended or twisted. I walk to my room's sealed steel exit-way tired like and show my face to the camera. It flashes bright good morning then speaks my name: Kovu, species: Human – rabbit hybrid pausing in between each word separating them.

The bars that lock this door way in place slide out after my identity is confirmed. The exit opens auto for me, and I step aside so that no injury comes from this potential mechanical violent attack. I walk through normal with my steps divided as I am always striving to be more human like. All motion-movement halted by me when I heard the lifeless announcement.

There were two time bombs until big explosion of me being late for my learning's. My heart was racing rapid with doubts of its winning. I began dashing like mad, turn corner left way, now right, up and jump down frightened stairs anticipating my fall, run zigzags, stop, stall, and wish for death.

My heart was no longer in the race, but now forfeit. I grabbed my chest as if trying to stop nervous pain from coming, and my white fur clenched under formal dress shirt. A fox with evil eyes and his friend the pig ignorant tiger had halted my on time attempt. I was in for the old double dose of brut torture that day. First from these monsters, and then the punishment the white coats had seen fit for me.

I looked through the space in between their two heads, and I could see teacher white coat glaring at me directly. He looked down at the time keeper attached to his wrist, and then looked mono-ops back at me with an even more disgusting expression that made me tremble. He was standing in front of the entrance to his room of lecture. I was so close to avoiding a much un-fit punishment even it was suited for a monster like me. The evil-eyed fox had such a nasty grin right before he grabbed me by the shoulders and pushed me to the cold steel floor. I struggled to get up as my arms flailing about.

"Now now, no need to fret and be all panic-like" the fox told me between his teeth still grinning all the while.

"That's right rabbit-freak, I'm sure your punishment will be more easy-like for the second go around" the tiger said all humor while happy-gobbling throughout. The tiger removed his custom dress shoe, put out his daily sharpened claws, and then to my chest he stomped. He then pulled his claws out of my chest which had gone at least a half inch or so deep causing my blood to rush out as if my body were a prison and the blood prisoner. I in turn squeak-screamed out which caused myself much shame and embarrassment.

The two monsters walked themselves to be greeted by teacher white coat. I was holding my chest trying to stop the blood from covering me completely, but it was no use, for my white fur was now a nasty red. Another artificial voice announcement: fifteen seconds until doors are to be closed. I began desperate crawling myself last attempt closer to the room of lecture with my fists clenched, and me now on my stomach, and I pushing myself while grunting and crying out. I was almost there and I was almost safe.

Yes, I was going to save myself, and it would be glorious. I had made it. I was about to slide myself through the door and leave my blood trail behind, but then there was loud death sound. My time had run out, teach standing above, his shoe before my face, I kicked outside, and then door slam.

I sat there for hours with my back against the cold steel wall. I had finally stopped bleeding, but my fur still stained. Somber sleep had begun its whispering in my ear, and my mind like shutdown ending all processes. A field of green grass, wind gently blowing, oh and the sun was stunning. Nothing I had read about in my books could even come close to such an amazing place as this. Science dismisses all religion, but if religion can give you such a place when you expire then I believe it all and I wish for death now.

I received something else instead, something worse than hell after death. The world stopped turning and was destroyed by the demons. My eyes were open, and I was being dragged across the path of judgment. I was sitting in the most uncomfortable steel chair, and my arms were already covered by needle holes. I couldn't much tell what horrible horror unfolded during my time in that torturous room, for my memory is faint. It must have been the drugs, but I do remember pain, and it was a nightmare I should never like to revisit.

I awoke the next day in my same old room. I hopped from my dream vessel and I didn't stop. I jumped and pounced from this end to the next. I kind of had some pre-adrenaline already going and I really was excited for today. Something about this was a little odd, but I didn't care too much at the time. I walked to my door and struggled to have patience, scan complete, identity confirmed, and then I went on. I ran so fast my eyes could not keep up, but this didn't matter because my brain was really fast that day and it knew the way by itself.

I ran into them again that fox and that tiger, but I didn't stop. I simply pushed them out of the way with ease and then entered my room of learning. I sat there and I smiled nice and wide with my feet still moving. Good day. Good day indeed.

Those two monsters walked in only shortly after I sat. They sat beside with one on each side of me. That was most uncomfortable; I sat there thinking into much anxiety. The teacher in white coat walked himself from the back to the front of the room all slow like. He wrote some numbers and some letters on the writing board, pointed to them, and said solve it like a real dictator would. I really was confused by this entire math and such. I was not interested in what numbers equaled this and what letters equaled that, but much more fascinated by that of the artists, the authors, the writers of history, fiction and fantasy. It was forbidden to look too much into these books, so I stole them while their eyes elsewhere, and their minds not attentive. I would take these books back to my room with me and study while confined and I had been doing this for years.

The voice of teacher drowned out by my own thinking, because I considered his to be without reason. I often found myself dreaming during the day, for inside our dream-vessels we did not dream, because our dreams were stolen from us while we just slept. I was outside of this place and freedom was beautiful. I looked with my virgin eyes so to see everything dancing around me. There was the whole world before me, and the world was perfect. Snap, snap, snap, his fingers went as teacher went all answer this, and answer that all spat spat spat in my face. I hadn't the slightest idea of what the questions were, and even if I did know and hadn't been day dreaming these past five minutes I would be more than just struggling to solve them. I sat there without any words, but I was still smiling with my two front teeth really sticking out which reminded me that they needed to be trimmed up and filed a bit since I had mostly been eating soft food.

"Well, it looks to me that you still haven't learned your lesson", the teacher said to me smirking.

TO BE CONTINUED

Two Sides

In one ear there is static
In the other painful reality
There are two sides with every life
On one side there is distorted truth
On the other there is painful reality

You can choose to throw away the senses, or
You can try to make sense of what is real
You can choose to forget it all, or
You can choose to remember everything, but
There will always be darkness within the light

Dear Empty Space,

I'm sorry I wasn't there when your mind caught fire
I'm sorry for not being able to feel what you felt
And I'm sorry for pretending like I were you
And saying that I understood

I wish I could step into your shoes
And then cry to you
And truly say that I am sorry
But until then these words are meaningless

The End of winter (Haiku)

The frozen ground melts
The clouds make way for the sun
Winter disappears

Gold Dreams

Dreams of being rich
Dreams of being famous
Dreams of a life
Just like the ones that you see
On the magazines and
On the T.V.
They all make it look so easy

A golden life
With everything gold
Hopes of reaching the top
Of the golden stairs
Only just to lay your golden crown down
After you get there
Gold dreams

Doorways

I am standing in a wide open field. The wind is blowing against me gently, and the field is completely empty. Nothing breathes but me. My eyes……are closed. I suddenly feel as if I am standing on nothing, oh but because there is no ground below my feet. I am not falling. I feel the urge to open my eyes so that I may see how this is possible. It is not possible. It has become unbelievable.

I want this to be real, and I want all that is not possible to connect with me. I want to be the impossible. I can no longer resist. My eyes are open. Darkness, yes total and complete darkness surrounds me. I can not see anything, and then there is light. Headlights, oh yes I know. Headlights on a car that is moving closer. The car is getting closer, and appears to have no intentions of stopping any time soon.

The car makes no noise at fist, and then I hear it. I hate this noise. It drives me to insanity. I want to destroy everything that this noise is, consume it and make it disappear. I feel nothing for this noise but pure absolute hatred. My paradise is about to be ripped away and there is nothing I can do to stop it.

The car has stopped moving. It is literally only a few feet away from me and appears to be frozen completely. The noise has not stopped, but I can see inside of the car. There is a shadowy figure in the driver's seat, and he is punching, beating violently at the horn on the steering wheel. An immensely bright light is shining into the car now. It is coming from a place unknown. I do not know where, but somebody is responsible, and I do not know who.

I can see the shadows face, as he continues to blow the horn and make that noise I hate. Oh this noise I can not stand, blast this noise, just blast it to hell will ye in control? I look at the shadow and he looks at me. I see myself and I wave goodbye.

I open my eyes a second time. I am in my room lying in the most loving bed as it holds me not wanting to ever let me go. I make myself get up, and I turn off the alarm clock. Most alarming indeed it is, but still oh whom ist in control blasts this noise for killing all my dreams even with them being as damn strange as they are. I laugh for a second or two, because the funny thing is I was never really asleep. I find unbearable pain in that this is actually humorous to me. I have been humiliated by my own mind. The world is collapsing, and so I open my door and I walk into the unknown. I am in a field.

The Museum

My eyes are open with everything is laid out clear before me, but it is my mind that is blurry. I can not remember how I came to be in this place, and this obscure state of mind I am in is all too extraneous for me to ignore. I raise myself from the cold wooden floor, stretch my unforgiving bones, and rub each eye separately to ensure full focus. I inspect my surroundings from a still position, and to add much more confusion and also some relief I find myself in what appears to be a museum. A museum, but why? – but I do not spend much time pondering on this. I start walking forward with my, “Hello, anyone there?” classic horror cliché echoing beside me and it running back and forth losing its breath with each of its times.

I hear nothing and everything seems to be absent of all life until a shadow is caught by my oh so weary but much anticipating eyes. The shadow is there just in front, just around the corner that hides the unknown; it is there peaking itself around as if it were a spy and it is to tell its owner of whom is coming. I up the speed of my steps, as I am eager to cure my curious disease and ready to encounter whatever devils may await my poor innocent soul.

I cross the corner, but it is strange and the way is empty. There are paintings all along this empty corridor of bliss waiting. They are all same scene, different character, and each with hands inviting. There is nothing that exists in this world except I as I walk down endlessly. I stop halfway, for this painting that I am now facing myself towards is different. It is moving, and when its eyes lock mine it starts whispering.

“Come forth”, it beckons me, “come forth”.

I do as it says because I have no choice, spellbound by the majesty of it all. The ghostly figure that once stood center painting is now gone. The painting is now only a blank canvas and as I walk into it a world is created. This is nothing, this is anything, everything. This is an empty entity, and this is a world created and destroyed a thousand times spanning countless years. I am inside of my own imagination.

Being Awake is a Nightmare

I want to go to sleep, but
There is still so much light outside
I ask my brain to turn it off
But it tells me no

I want to stop thinking
I try and tell myself that it is safe
And that nothing can hurt me
But my brain isn't convinced

I let myself go
I have no control
These thoughts keep spinning
And they hold me down

A Standing Still Tree

Holding on
When I just want to let go
And be free
Just let everything go

A standing still tree
Has only leaves that move
But only when the wind blows
Time freezes unexpectedly

Now the world has stopped turning
And everything is still
But nothing has changed for me
My mind is the only thing left alive

The Box

There is a box floating out at sea
The creator sent it off
Hoping it would reach me
But he just watches aloft

This box is the cure to every problem
If it arrived and made my mind tranquil
I would have a choice in being solemn
And I would forever be thankful

Waiting Still

I wait like a tree
Whose leaves are waiting for the wind
I wait because I can't see
And am afraid of the end

I wait like the message bottle
Who is being carried by the ocean
I wait like the role model
Who has stopped all motion

I wait because the world is impatient
I wait because if I woke up
I wouldn't be able to take it
I wait like a lost pup

Happiness

Happy?
I often wonder this myself
Happy?
No I don't need your help
Happy?
Right now I wish for everyone to be

Happy?
Amongst the chaos of tonight
Happy?
I know what's wrong and what's right
Happy?
Right now I wish for everyone to be

Falling Forward

Hiding sun never left the grave
Some skeletons never change
Falling forward with arms reaching out
There is no standing when it isn't allowed

My Own Prison

If only it were different
Oh how I wish it would change
But nothing is different
And nothing has changed
I am spinning down
And out of control
Further and further down I go
Sinking deeper and deeper
Until I am finally buried alive
There is nowhere I can go
The prison has already been built
And the doors already locked

A Lucid Dream

I have never walked this way before and why is it so empty of life? I kept walking until my knees weak and I to the floor. I looked into this mirror with me now on my knees. This mirror, oh this horrid mirror, where did it come from all of the sudden? Or how did it get here in front me rather? It had me in a daze gazing into it confused by whom I really was. Why was my reflection not clear? I thought into a thought that soon consumed me. The reflection of me that the mirror displayed was clear now, and it was me, but I was……? I awoke and my eyes gave unto me the gift of reality displayed in beautiful color.

The dream was still puzzling to me, was that what it was like to have a lucid dream? I shouldn't have looked into the mirror.

Just Clothing

Both eyebrows and questions rose
The second their eyes had caught sight
Of the clothing that she had chose
And so up up up with his or her nose
But she simply passed them on her way
And surpassed them with all that she knows

The Glass Angel

The glass angel was standing high
It always seemed to be watching over you
As you passed it by
The angel's life had ended
As I fell
It descended
Its wings torn apart
How do I apologize?
Where do I start?
How do you replace something that meant so much?
I am sorry
But I know that isn't enough

Ice Angel

The ice trimmed
With perfect cold
Lanterns waiting
To welcome heaven
Snow descending
To remind the forgotten
Glass cut into perfection
Would rather not shatter
But instead melt and
Become the rain that falls
So it may once again
Sail the skies
From cloud to cloud
From eye to eye

Admiring Nature

The lion that hunts, captures, and kills its prey. It is the same lion that sometimes seems as if it sleeps all day. The families of lions wander from place to place in search of food, but sometimes stop to play along the way. We can watch from a far and compare them to some human families by the way that the mother provides and tries to teach her cubs, so that one day they can provide for their families. Oh, but of coarse nature is beautiful, and we will always desire a connection with it. This is the majesty of it all, for we must hold ourselves back, and we must understand that such amazing creatures should be left to their own environment, and can only be admired in this way.

Love Lost

Ones love lost and left
While the other still stays
A heart once warm and red
Now cold and grey
Begging for a safe passage home
But instead losing myself deeper
Into the unknown
One must first find himself
And one must refuse
Any kind of help
That day will surely come
When love
No longer has to run

The Dark Days

The days that once let in light
Are now the days that reject it
I have become the days
As they have consumed me
And the days have become me

The days are darkened as soon as I arrive
I bring the days an unpleasant welcome
But the days must understand
That I can not leave
And neither can the days

Hidden Footprints

I think there is a place I must go
A path I must follow
The way is there for me
But it is hidden

Many have taken this path before me
And they have left their footprints behind
For me to follow
But they are hidden

Hidden in places I can not search
Hidden in ways that I can't understand
Hidden oh yes hidden
Hidden where I will never find them

-

The Old Cat

We watched this cat grow
From an energetic and playful kitten
To an old and weak bake-neko
And then we were afraid

It was the lamp oil it would drink
It was its tail that was too long
Or maybe it had just grown too old
We don't really know for sure

We all saw it fly away
It went from weak to strong
We still wonder where it went to
But at night I sometimes see it

The World From Above

I can see the world out there
It is oh so colorful
I can see the world out there
It is oh so wonderful

When I try to enter
It all comes down on me
When I try to enter
There is nothing I can't see

The Dirt

We all trample on the dirt
We all walk around on it
We walk like we own the dirt
But the dirt is laughing at us

It is laughing away
As we stomp its face
It is laughing away
As it's being kicked

Because one day the dirt will own us
And we will no longer be walking
But lying helpless as the dirt consumes us
And has its revenge

Breathing is blind

You have to wake up
Before you see
You have to start walking
Before you leave

If you can't breathe
Then you can't see
And if you can't see
Then you're just blind

The Beginning of the Great War

It was a very bright morning in the kingdom of Caelum. The flying serpents were resting breathless and motionless and even Sir Gigas was as peaceful as the stagnant night watcher. Pater Sunshine was responsible for such a bright good morning as he himself made this very obvious by his boasting and his loud laughter, for when he would open his mouth all the light came pouring out all glorious. His voice went ringing so far as to be believed by some to have even reached the humans.

"Oh and how I am the victor again and again and again!", Pater Sunshine exclaimed with much joy and pride. There is no one who can kill me, not even in my sleep, and especially not Dominus Dark out of all the immortals. "Hahahahowhowha", Pater Sunshine started into another deep laugh.

Yes, all was well in the kingdom of Caelum, and everyone and everything was at peace. However, just hours before, while it was still night it was a much different scene. Dominus Dark had decided that having the night belong to him was not enough, and so he decided to leave his home of darkness and chaos and travel to the kingdom of Caelum where there he had planned on taking the head of Vater Sunshine and with it the day to control as his. He had wanted to fill every day with total and complete darkness and destroy every bit of light that ever existed. Vater Sunshine was sleeping at the time when Dominus Dark had planned on killing him, but right before Dominus Dark swung his dreadful ax Vater Sunshine awoke with a mighty thunderous roar that knocked Dominus Dark down from the top of Caelum and falling down to what Vater Sunshine thought to be his death.

Vater Sunshine didn't know why Dominus Dark wanted him dead, but he was too overwhelmed by his joyous victory to even care. He was still laughing away with his eyes now barely open and bright golden tears raining down from his face. During this proud state he was in he did not take any notice to Dominus Dark who had climbed himself back up to the top of Caelum. Dominus Dark had slowly crept his way until he was standing just behind Vater Sunshine who sat tall and still laughing. Dominus Dark grinned such a nasty evil grin as he readied his giant ax by gripping it firmly and holding it just inches away from Vater Sunshines neck.

"I won, you've lost!", Dominus Dark shouted menacingly. Vater Sunshine heard this, but before he had the chance to turn himself around Dominus Dark raised his ax high above and then swung with all his might. There was no longer any laughing. No, there was not a sound to be heard after that. Vater Sunshines head went flying into the dark abyss that was slowly starting to cover everything. There was no blood, but instead an immensely bright light was shining straight up into the sky from Vater Sunshines neck, and in the center of the light was an omega symbol as if it were a signal for something.

Dominus Dark saw this and grew furious. He tried to cover the light with his darkness, but no matter how hard he tried, the light that was shining up into the sky was still as bright as ever, and the omega symbol still there in the center signaling something. It was a signal for the Great War that was to follow.

Lost and Amidst Falling Stairs

I traveled
And I fell
I mattered
And I stepped forward

I wanted more
Until I wanted nothing
I wanted to soar
But now I'm melting

Take this and hide it away
Take this and hide it away
Take this and hide it
So I will never find it

Questioning the Sky

Where do we go?
Now that everything is gone
Everything that we once loved
Now gone away

What do we do?
When the wind comes for us
Everything that we once knew
Now blown away

We run away with our voices high
We run so fast
That we can cry with the angels
And then we wait until the new day rises

The Dead King

The king cast the first stone
The stone was thrown
From the now empty throne
The king was forced to leave
He could no longer do as he pleased
All of the angels dropped to their knees
The people waved goodbye
While a marksman kept an open eye
And that was the day that the king died

The Rabbit

The rabbit wandered away
Now searching through the empty days
Creating a path for one to follow
Traveling through a world so hollow

When the clock is running this fast
One has to wonder how long time will last
But the rabbit runs faster
Running to its master

www.ingramcontent.com/pod-product-compliance
Ingram Content Group UK Ltd.
Pitfield, Milton Keynes, MK11 3LW, UK
UKHW051133260726
13967UKWH00010B/3029